The TOOTH Book

By
Theo. LeSieg

Illustrated by
Roy McKie

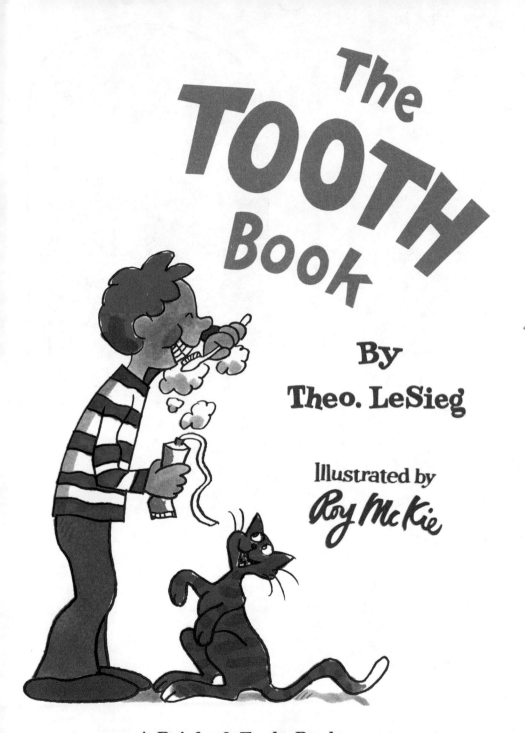

A Bright & Early Book

From BEGINNER BOOKS
A Division of Random House, Inc., New York

Who has teeth?

Well . . .
look around
and you'll find out who.
You'll find
that red-headed uncles do.

Policemen do.
And zebras too.

And unicycle riders do.

And camels
and their drivers do!

Even little girls named Ruthie
all have teeth.
All Ruths are toothy.

Teeth!
You find them everywhere!
On mountaintops!
And in the air!

And if you care
to poke around,
you'll even find them
underground.

You'll find them
east, west, north, and south.
You'll find them
in a lion's mouth.

TEETH!
They are very much in style.

They must be
very much
worthwhile!

"They come in handy
when you chew,"
says Mr. Donald Driscoll Drew.

"That's why
my family
grew a few."

"They come in handy when you smile," says Smiling Sam the crocodile.

"They come in handy
in my job,"
says high trapezer
Mike McCobb.

"If I should ever
lose a tooth,
I'd lose my wife.
And that's the truth."

"Teeth come in handy when you speak," says news broadcaster Quincy Queek.

"Without my teeth
I'd talk like ducks,
and only broadcast
quacks and klucks."

"You're lucky
that you have your teeth,"
says a sad, sad snail
named Simon Sneeth.

"I don't have one!
I can never smile
like Smiling Sam the crocodile."

"Clams have no teeth,"
says Pam the clam.
"I cannot eat
hot dogs
or ham."

"No teeth at all,"
says Pam the clam.
"I cannot eat
roast leg of lamb.
Or peanuts! Pizzas!
Popcorn! SPAM!
Not even huckleberry jam!"

"Without teeth
we can't play trombones,"
says a jellyfish named Jimbo Jones.

"I have no teeth,"
says Hilda Hen.
"But women do.
And so do men.

"So I have happy
news for you.
You will grow two sets!
Set one. Set two."

"You will lose
set number one.
And when you do,
it's not much fun.

"But then you'll grow
set number two!
32 teeth, and all brand new.
16 downstairs, and 16 more
upstairs on the upper floor.

"And when you get your second set,
THAT'S ALL THE TEETH
YOU'LL EVER GET!"

SO . . .
don't chew down trees
like beavers do.
If you try,
you'll lose set
number two!

And . . .
don't be dumb
like Mr. Glotz.
Don't break your teeth
untying knots!

And don't be dumb
like Katy Klopps.
Don't try to chew off
bottle tops!

Don't gobble junk
like Billy Billings.
They say his teeth
have fifty fillings!

They sure are handy
when you smile.
So keep your teeth
around awhile.

And <u>never</u> bite your dentist
when he works inside your head.

Your dentist is
your teeth's best friend.

Bite carrot sticks instead!

THEO. LESIEG is almost as well known to beginning readers as his mentor, Dr. Seuss. They both write wonderful stories that delight and entertain millions of children the world over. But, whereas Dr. Seuss also illustrates the stories he writes, Theo. LeSieg likes to have someone else draw the pictures for his books. And his favorite artist is Roy McKie.

ROY MCKIE is famous all over the world for his happy, brilliant pictures for picture books. Some of the most popular books he has drawn the pictures for are the Beginner Books *My Book About Me*, *Ten Apples Up On Top*, and Bennett Cerf's *Animal Riddles*. The last book Roy illustrated was another funny Bright and Early, *The Hair Book*.